Naturalism And The Superman In The Novels Of

Jack London

Charles Child Walcutt

[Reprinted from PAPERS OF THE MICHIGAN ACADEMY OF SCIENCE, ARTS AND LETTERS, Vol. XXIV, Part IV, 1938. Published 1939]

NATURALISM AND THE SUPERMAN IN THE NOVELS OF JACK LONDON

CHARLES CHILD WALCUTT

ANYONE who investigates the ramifications of literary naturalism in the American novel will at some time be confronted with the problem of the "superman" — a creature of whom there are almost as many conceptions as there are fictional representatives. It is my purpose here to attempt to distinguish between these various concepts of the superman, to show their relation to the naturalistic tradition, and to explore some of the ethical implications which are curiously associated with a sort of naturalism in the work of Jack London.

Naturalism appears in a novel when the philosophy of materialistic monism is somehow applied to its conception or execution. The perfectly naturalistic novel would be one in which the action is completely determined by material forces — economic, social, physiological. For this condition to exist a corollary requirement with respect to the characters in the novel must be fulfilled: they too must be explained in terms of purely material causation, and they must be so completely explained in these terms that impressions of free will and ethical responsibility do not intrude to disrupt the relentless operation of this material causation. In practice, however, the principle of determinism has never been able entirely to supplant the everyday belief in ethical freedom upon which all our reactions to the conduct of others are based. Plots, furthermore, have in the past been constructed around personal conflicts and choices which always depend for their importance upon the assumption of free will and ethical responsibility in the actors. Hence a study of naturalism in the novel may resolve itself into a study of how and to what degree the philosophy of materialism has, with respect to structure and characterization, replaced this ethical attitude toward the judgment of human affairs.

In Jack London's novels there is a clash of sober ideas, emotional

89

convictions, and attitudes that come from London the writer of popular stories rather than from London the social and philosophical thinker. To explain the kind of naturalism, if there is any, which appears in his novels it will be convenient to consider the ideas which grew both from his experience and from his reading. This material will, when seen in relation to the exigencies involved in writing for the sort of people to whom London wished to appeal, constitute a basis for the discussion of such naturalistic elements as we may find in his writings.

The painful and brutal events[1] of London's life in the years before he began to write are reflected in most of his early works.[2] It is significant that the material of these books is derived from actual experience, for, as we shall see, this experience modified and conditioned London's reaction to his readings in philosophy and science. He was able to rise above the hard conditions of his early life; and the fact that he gloried in the memory of his youthful adventures shows to some extent how he himself embodied the positive exuberance and vitality which he celebrated so often in his stories. His temperament, in short, led him to a romantic glorification of strength and bravery. He saw everything from farming to fighting in heroic terms. He even fought with his ideas, and it seems likely that his personality more than his early experiences caused him to search out brutality and, subsequently, to exploit it in his novels. A weakling, for example, would never have shipped on a sealing vessel at the age of seventeen. This heroic side of London's character is not without its ludicrous aspects: he could not help being self-conscious about his manliness; and the most determined admirer of Jack London must smile at such a passage as the following, quoted from his wife's biography of him:

> George S[t]erling had affectionately dubbed him "The Wolf," or "The Fierce Wolf," or "The Shaggy Wolf." In the last month of Jack London's life, he gave me an exquisite tiny wrist-watch. "And what shall I have engraved on it?" I asked. "Oh, 'Mate from Wolf,' I guess," he replied. And I:

[1] Before he was twenty-one he had worked in a cannery, been a hobo, a drunkard, and an oyster pirate, had shipped on a long sealing cruise, and had followed the gold rush to the Yukon. See *Martin Eden*, 1909; *John Barleycorn*, 1913; and the life by Charmian London, *The Book of Jack London* (New York 1921. 2 vols.).

[2] A complete list of London's writings, with dates of publication, appears in the Appendix to the *Book of Jack London*, II : 397–414. The present study will consider only two or three representative novels, but in some detail.

"The same as when we exchanged engagement watches?" "Why, yes, if you don't mind," he admitted. "I have sometimes wished you would call me 'Wolf' more often." [3]

This ridiculous bit of dialogue illustrates what appears everywhere in the biography: that London was drawing a real or fancied portrait of himself in Sea-Wolf Larsen and in most of his other "primitive" and strong-minded heroes.

The philosophy which London evolved from his life and reading can be defined fairly easily, for he repeated his beliefs at every possible opportunity, in both social and literary utterance. He had read parts of Herbert Spencer's *Synthetic Philosophy* before he was twenty-one,[4] and Spencer's influence seems never to have waned. As a Spencerian he became a complete materialist, writing that "The different families of man must yield to law — to LAW, inexorable, blind, unreasoning law, which has no knowledge of good or ill, right or wrong." [5]   Again, he writes in 1900 that

John Fiske has done many queer gymnastics in order to reconcile Spencer, whose work he worships, to his own beliefs in immortality and God. But he doesn't succeed very well. He jumps on Haeckel, with both feet, but in my modest opinion, Haeckel's position is as yet unassailable.[6]

That this materialism was no passing fancy may be demonstrated by quotation of a statement of belief that he wrote fifteen years later:

I am a hopeless materialist. I see the soul as nothing else than the sum of the activities of the organism plus personal habits, memories, and experiences of the organism, plus inherited habits, memories, experiences, of the organism. *I believe that when I am dead, I am dead.* . . . .
I have no patience with the metaphysical philosophers. With them, always, the wish is parent to the thought, and their wish is parent to their profoundest philosophical conclusions.[7]

The idealism of the transcendentalists, of John Fiske and Josiah Royce, the pragmatic idealism of William James, and the poetic

---

[3] *Book of Jack London*, II : 72.

[4] *Ibid.*, I : 238.   In 1899 he writes: "Knowing no God, I have made man my worship; and surely I have learned how vile he can be." *Ibid.*, I : 284. He is "an evolutionist, believing in Natural Selection, half believing in Malthus' 'Law of Population,' and a myriad other factors thrown in." *Ibid.*, I : 285. In the same letter he reflects his reading of Spencer's *First Principles* by exclaiming: "If people could come to realize the utter absurdity, logically, of the finite contemplating the infinite." *Ibid.*, I : 286; see also I : 296.

[5] *Ibid.*, I : 297, from a letter to Cloudsley Johns, a friend in whom London confided frequently.

[6] *Ibid.*, I : 331.   [7] Quoted from a letter of 1914, *ibid.*, I, facing p. 304.

idealism of Whitman may be considered products of the American frontier. They express the spirit of a nation that had grown for more than two hundred years with free land in the West. By 1900 London, as we have just seen, could scorn the idealism of Fiske and other metaphysicians. But the spirit of American democracy, still strong within him, found an outlet which was equally idealistic and equally representative of the American spirit. Thus coexisting with his determinism and justified perhaps by his faith in Darwin — though the logical relation is not perfectly clear — is London's belief in the importance of racial integrity. To him the mixed breed of any sort is weak and useless, and of all the "pure" breeds the Anglo-Saxon is the best.

God [he proclaims] abhors a mongrel. In nature there is no place for a mixed breed. . . . Consult the entire history of the human world in all past ages, and you will find that the world has ever belonged to the pure breed and has never belonged to the mongrel.[8]

This love of the pure breed is of a piece with London's love of the strong man; it is also obscurely related to his faith in evolution — as if survival and racial mixture were incompatible — and it is in a sense idealistic.

Although London was unshakably attached to his materialism and could write that "man is not a free agent, and free will [as the power of ethical choice] is a fallacy exploded by science long ago," [9] he was equally sure of the truth of Darwin's ideas about the struggle for existence; and the latter belief, since it indicated that survival depended upon superior force or guile, led him inevitably to the conviction that his will (as vital impulse or force) was the one positive *fact* upon which an individual could base his actions. In glorifying strength, that is, he glorified the *will* (as vital force) which seems always to exist in a character — whether real or imaginary — who has superior cunning or power. The ability to triumph in a struggle argues the ability to exercise one's power; and the latter *determination* is identified as a will. "A strong will," he writes, "can accomplish anything." [10] The difference between absolute materialism, on the one hand, and a belief in will and self-assertion as the only workable guides of conduct, on the other, is merely one of attitude. The former is the conclusion of the philosopher who views the struggle calmly from without and considers its implications in

[8] *Book of Jack London,* I : 297–298.   [9] *Ibid.,* I : 369.   [10] *Ibid.,* I : 284.

absolute terms. The latter is the belief of the same philosopher when he becomes personally involved in the struggle and evaluates its implications with reference to his own pleasure and pain: he knows that his sensations are real and he acts upon his impulse to make them pleasant ones.[11] Thus in effect he considers what, philosophically, he knows as vital impulse, to have for his own purposes the power of ethical choice — for to him his impulses are *good*.

The materialistic ideas and the red-blooded temperament that have been described here go in a peculiar way into London's writings. One critic describes the combination as a union of evolutionary belief with the thrill of his own struggle:

London, with the strength of the strong, exulted in the struggle for survival. He saw human history in terms of the evolutionary dogma, which to him seemed a glorious, continuous epic of which his stories were episodes. He set them in localities where the struggle would be most obvious: in the wilds of Alaska, on remote Pacific Islands, on ships at sea out of hearing of the police.[12]

These epics of survival require rugged and combative heroes — men who can thrive in a struggle where physical prowess is of the first importance. Having brutes for heroes and setting the struggle for existence beyond the controls of civilization is an obvious falsification of the conditions of human evolution. Man is a social creature, and to be studied scientifically he should be studied in society. But sociology does not provide such thrilling materials for fiction as do these heroic conflicts on the frontier.

From this recognition of the sort of hero that London chose to exploit in his novels we may turn to a consideration of the superman. London's heroes are said to be supermen,[13] and the superman must be cornered and identified before we can proceed to show his place in London's naturalism, for his "naturalism," his determinism, and

[11] In two letters written a little over a week apart and to the same person London expresses his beliefs in materialism, determinism, socialism, the importance of racial purity, and "the thrill of life" that comes from asserting oneself in the struggle for existence. *Ibid.*, I : 295–297. This is a good example of the way all these ideas can coexist in a single intellect without striking incongruity or confusion.

[12] Van Doren, Carl, *The American Novel* (New York, 1931), p. 268. London wrote in the heyday of the Rooseveltian "strenuous life" — a concept that was highly "ethical."

[13] "In every country, writers like Jack London were choosing supermen for their heroes." Hartwick, Harry, *The Foreground of American Fiction* (New York, 1934), p. 79.

his use of so-called supermen are all products of the same complex of ideas.

From the point of view of one critic the brute superman is a product of despair. He is developed, according to Mr. Harry Hartwick, by the writer who abandons ethical control and substitutes impulse for intellection in his portrayal of nature's brutal creed. "The naturalist," he says, defining the outlook of the writer who is afflicted with this despair,

lets Nature take its course .... [To him] Nature is a vast contrivance of wheels within wheels; man is a "piece of fate" caught in the machinery of Nature; and love is ultimately a product of the same forces that control gravitation. .... Man's only duty is to discharge his energies and die, at the same time expressing his individuality as best he can.[14]

The writer burdened with this attitude, says Mr. Hartwick, creates a superman and, according to his creed of *laissez faire* (by which Hartwick means rampant individualism), allows him to fight out his own savage destiny. Now this analysis rests upon several different concepts of what a superman is, and we may perhaps arrive most easily at a full understanding of the connotations of the word by distinguishing these several concepts.

The Nietzschean superman, to begin at the fountainhead, is the apotheosis of individualism. He is selfish, cunning, amoral, achieving happiness through the fullest indulgence of his will to power.[15] All those ethical ideas which teach a man to deny himself and to restrain his impulses as fundamentally evil are the doctrines preached by weaklings in their efforts to protect themselves from the strong. These are the tenets of "slave morality." Nietzsche exhorted the strong to be guided by "master morality." Uplifting the weak is a profitless business and will, in the long run, degrade the race. The self-development of the superman, on the other hand, will lead to progress, for it will effect the elimination of the unfit and the consequent purification of humanity. In this latter notion we see the

[14] *The Foreground of American Fiction*, pp. 17–18.
[15] See Mencken, H. L., *The Philosophy of Friedrich Nietzsche* (London, 1908), pp. 103 f. See also Berg, Leo, *The Superman in Modern Literature* (London [1915]); de Casseres, B., *The Superman in America*, University of Washington Chapbooks, Number 30 (Seattle, 1929); Wright, W. H., *What Nietzsche Taught* (New York, 1917); and Nietzsche's *Also Sprach Zarathustra* (1885), *Jenseits von Gute und Böse* (1886), *Zur Genealogie der Moral* (1887), and the unfinished *Die Wille zur Macht*. Nietzsche's works were little known in America before 1900 (see p. 95, n. 17).

element in Nietzsche's thought which, related to science and Darwinism, seeks not just anarchical egoism but the constant improvement
and progress that one could infer to be the results of evolution if its
operation were not impeded by the folly of slave morality, which
preserves the unfit.　It is this very idea, furthermore, which raises
the genuine superman far above a mere ruthless brute who triumphs
over his competitors by sheer force.　The highest superman, indeed,
was to surpass present man as completely as man surpasses the ape.
As Mencken explains,

> Nietzsche, it will be observed, was unable to give any very definite picture
> of this proud, heaven-kissing superman.　It is only in Zarathustra's preachments
> to "the higher man," a sort of bridge between man and superman, that we may
> discern the philosophy of the latter.　On one occasion Nietzsche penned a passage
> which seemed to compare the superman to "the great blond beasts" which ranged
> Europe in the days of the mammoth, and from this fact many commentators
> have drawn the conclusion that he had in mind a mere two-legged brute, with
> none of the higher traits that we now speak of as distinctly human.　But, as a
> matter of fact, he harbored no such idea.　In another place, wherein he speaks
> of three metamorphoses of the race, under the allegorical names of the camel,
> the lion and the child, he makes this plain.　The camel, a hopeless beast of burden,
> is man.　But when the camel goes into the solitary desert, it throws off its burden
> and becomes a lion.　That is to say, the heavy and hampering load of artificial
> dead-weight called morality is cast aside and the instinct to live — or, as Nietzsche
> insists upon regarding it, the will to power, — is given free rein.　The lion is the
> "higher man" — the intermediate stage between man and superman.　The
> latter appears neither as camel nor lion, but as a little child.　He knows a little
> child's peace.　He has a little child's calm.　Like a babe *in utero*, he is ideally
> adapted to his environment.[16]

Nietzsche's conception of the superman was not widely known in
America until after 1905.[17]　Up to that time there were in our litera-

---

[16] *Philosophy of Friedrich Nietzsche*, pp. 112–113.

[17] See de Casseres, *The Superman in America*, p. 15.　*The Reader's Guide*
between 1897 and 1907 lists thirty articles on Nietzsche — only three a year.
Shaw's *Man and Superman* (1905), Mencken's *Philosophy of Friedrich Nietzsche*
(1908), and James Huneker's *Egoists: A Book of Supermen* (1909) brought the
word and many of Nietzsche's ideas into this country and before the eyes of the
popular reader.　Nietzsche's works were not generally accessible in translation
at the turn of the century, although a number of them had been translated.
Mügge, M. A., *Friedrich Nietzsche: His Life and Work* (London, 1908), gives
an extensive bibliography in which are listed the following English editions:
The Case of Wagner, tr. Thomas Common (London, 1896, 1899) (contains *The
Twilight of the Idols* and *The Antichrist*); *Thus Spake Zarathustra: A Book for
All and None*, tr. Alexander Tille (London, 1896, 1899); *A Genealogy of Morals*.
Poems, tr. W. A. Haussmann and John Gray (London, 1897, 1899); *The Dawn
of Day*, tr. Johanna Volz (London, 1903); *Beyond Good and Evil*, tr. Helen
Zimmern (London, 1907); *Human, All-Too-Human*, Chapters I–III, tr. A. Har-

ture a number of manifestations which have been mistakenly called supermen by critics of a later date. There is, first, the physical giant who emerges when a writer portrays the struggle for existence on the frontier or the sea — under conditions where social restraints are removed and the victory of physical "survival values" may be most effectively displayed. Under such conditions the writer may choose for a hero the "blond beast" whom later critics have called a superman. This combination of pseudo science and the romantic quest for new materials does not, however, produce a Nietzschean superman.[18]

Science leads to the creation of supermen in another, quite different way: The naturalist has had new fields opened to him by the right which science assumes to explore all areas of thought and being. These new fields contain many horrible and disgusting subjects which the naturalist can exploit and render doubly affecting by his ostensibly scientific approach to them. Partly through his concern with such striking material, and partly through his desire to employ the deterministic outlook in his work, the naturalist is led to write about sociological extremes, for it is in the sordid side of life that the operation of external force upon man is most satisfactorily displayed. When the higher ethical nature of man is either denied or ignored, the emphasis must perforce be placed upon the physical, racial, instinctive, brutal side. There is no alternative. People who have no spiritual values are by the same token sure to be moved by physical compulsions. They can of course be purely the objects of

---

vey (Chicago, 1908). The first complete translation of Nietzsche's works, edited by Oscar Levy, was issued between 1909 and 1914. Toward 1910 critical books, such as J. M. Kennedy's *The Quintessence of Nietzsche* (New York, 1910) and A. Ludovici's *Nietzsche and Art* (Boston, 1912), appeared.

[18] But many people thought it did: as late as 1917 the notion prevails in an article by L. S. Friedland, "Jack London as Titan," *The Dial*, 62 (Jan. 25, 1917): 49–51. Mr. Friedland deplores the Russians' adoration of London, deeming tragic "that strange twist in their 'idealism' which makes them identify life with visible action and outer victory, with the superman, — brief master of all but himself" — and concludes that the finest deeds "will need a balance and sanity, an inner health and nobility for which the hurried superman of action has not time to wait" (p. 51). The writer in these last words more or less defines the Nietzschean superman when apparently he means to describe a higher being than "the hurried superman of action." He uses the word superman to describe the physical giant, not, as he should, the man of "inner health and nobility." This physical giant comes from a union of Darwinism and romance which seeks the most obvious field wherein to demonstrate the nature and operation of "survival values" of the crudest sort.

force; but if they move themselves their characters must contain strong emotional urges. Now the sociological cases of, say, Zola's *L'Assommoir* are represented as mostly animal, in order that Zola may study their reactions to their environment in the simplest terms — unhampered, that is, by any exalted spiritual yearnings in them, which would be most difficult to analyze as products of heredity or milieu. In Zola's novels such creatures are part of a larger whole, they are more or less explained by their environments, and their actions frequently take place within a broad cycle of movement that depends upon the external deterministic forces whose operation Zola attempts to study. *Remove the large sociological framework* and you have the atavistic, red-blooded brute who makes such wonderful material for stirring romance. To call such a creature a superman is a mistake. Rather he is instinctive, physical man set free to roam at large in terrific conflicts outside the restraining influences of society. He is not capable of endless conquest under all conditions. Indeed he is ill-fitted to triumph in the struggle for existence of civilized society. He has little in common with the superman described by Nietzsche. But he is physically strong; the naïve transition from a creature who is only physical to one who is strong physically is quite understandable, though not therefore reasonable; and in a world where strength counts he will flourish until cunning or accident destroy him.

Another kind of superbrute dates back to Greek myth, to Norse saga, or indeed to any of the heroic literatures that derive from periods when physical prowess was the most important survival value. The tradition of celebrating valor is perpetuated — regardless of an author's knowledge of Darwin or determinism — whenever a story is laid upon the frontier, where law does not successfully inhibit the acquisitive instincts, where only the comparatively strong or adventurous come in the first place, and where, consequently, success depends upon physical power rather than intellectual vision.[19]

[19] Norris's interest in saga literature has been noticed by Franklin Walker, *Frank Norris: A Biography* (New York, 1932), p. 163. The importance of the frontier in directing writers' attention toward such characters cannot be over-estimated. Heroic literatures, with their characteristic giantism, have always described or sprung from frontier conditions. The prevalence of such conditions in the American West until close to 1900 would account for the appearance of any number of physical giants or strong men whose creators knew nothing of science, Darwin, or Nietzsche. In practice, however, we shall see that the heroic and the "materialistic" motives were usually combined.

Still another kind of superman arises from a preoccupation with what has been called primordialism. It is the exploitation of the fact that civilization is a thin veneer and that the primitive brute is close to the surface in everyone. Combine this primordialism with the sort of exultation over physical strength that London manifests and there results the "Call-of-the-Wild" school of fiction, upon which F. T. Cooper has commented as follows:

> There is a vast difference between thinking of man as a healthy human animal and thinking of him as an unhealthy human beast. . . . The chief trouble with all the so-called Back-to-Nature books is that they suggest an abnormal self-consciousness, a constant preoccupation regarding the measure of our animalism. Now, it is a sort of axiom that so long as we are healthy and normal, we do not give much thought to our physical machinery. . . . But this, in a certain way, is precisely what the characters in the average Call-of-the-Wild novel seem to be doing. . . . They seem, so to speak, to keep their fingers insistently upon the pulse of their baser animal emotions, — and this is precisely what the primitive, healthy savage is furthest removed from doing.[20]

In this labyrinth of paths to the rugged brutes exalted by London the conception of the superman presented by Nietzsche is lost. That is, Nietzsche's writings cannot be said to account for all such creatures who appear in the American novel around the turn of the century. Yet all such creatures (with the possible exception of pure heroic types) spring from a single complex of ideas that formed about materialism, Darwinism, and science; and although many of them exhibit, because they are looking at the struggle *from within*, states of mind which do not make any active use of the concept of determinism, their ultimate relation to the materialism which begets that determinism will be clear to anyone who has followed the analysis thus far. It should also be clear that what prevents the various brutes described here from being Nietzschean supermen is, primarily, that they embody no ideal of perfection, that they are not conceived as being a step in the direction of progress.

We have seen that the supermen of adventure novels do not necessarily owe much to Nietzsche but that they do have affiliations with the naturalistic philosophy. Our next problem is to see how completely London was able to pattern his novels upon his avowed materialism — to see, in short, whether the ethics of Christianity ever became confused with the survival ethics of an absolute materialist.

[20] "Primordialism and Some Recent Books," *The Bookman*, 30 (1909) : 278. Here is a shrewd recognition of London's concern with his own manliness.

It has been said that a writer puts most of himself into his early work, and the statement is strikingly true of London's first novel, *A Daughter of the Snows* (1902). He subsequently lamented that he had squandered in it material enough for a dozen novels.[21] The procedure in this analysis will be to present some of the ideas in *A Daughter of the Snows* and to consider the functional relation between the deterministic or naturalistic ideology that we uncover and the structural pattern of the novel. Beginning, then, with the ideas, we find a wealth of exposition that sets forth most of the beliefs which have been discussed earlier in this paper.

The operation of determinism is presented in the clearest terms, although with rather elaborate pedantry.[22] But hard on the heels of this exposition comes a belief in primordialism — the belief that man resists external pressures most gloriously when he is nearest the primitive state.

Thus, in the young Northland [he writes], frosty and grim and menacing, men stripped off the sloth of the south and gave battle greatly. And they stripped likewise much of the veneer of civilization — all of its follies, most of its foibles, and perhaps a few of its virtues. Maybe so; but they reserved the great traditions and at least lived frankly, laughed honestly, and looked one another in the eyes.[23]

Elsewhere this creed is expanded in a defense of atavism — of the notion that one's adaptability (and therefore one's likelihood of survival) depends upon one's nearness to a primitive state. The hero's

greatest virtue lay in this: he had not become hardened in the mould baked by his several forbears. . . . Some atavism had been at work in the making of him . . . . But so far this portion of his heritage had lain dormant. He had simply remained adjusted to a stable environment. . . . But whensoever the call came, being so constituted, it was manifest that he should adapt, should adjust himself to the unwonted pressure of new conditions. The maxim of the rolling stone may be all true; but notwithstanding, in the scheme of life, the inability to become fixed is an excellence par excellence.[24]

---

[21] *Book of Jack London*, I : 384.

[22] "Each [man] is the resultant of many forces which go to make a pressure mightier than he, and which moulds [*sic*] him in the predestined shape. But, with sound legs under him, he may run away, and meet with a new pressure. He may continue running, each new pressure prodding him as he goes, until he dies, and his final form will be that predestined of the many pressures." *A Daughter of the Snows* (ed. London, 1908), pp. 201–202.

[23] *Ibid.*, p. 202.

[24] *Ibid.*, p. 76. In *The Call of the Wild* (1903) Buck's fitness is measured by his primordialism, by the way "he [a dog] was harking back through his own life

With such an outlook one would expect London to set forth as survival values the cruder kinds of physical might and brute courage; and that is just what he does, but he presents them with the self-consciousness and muscle-flexing self-idolatry of one who is bent upon attaching high spiritual values to brute force. The emphasis in the following passage upon body, body, body — upon those muscles of which your true primitive man is wholly unconscious — is typical of this attitude toward the struggle for existence and toward the kind of beings he would like to see prevail. Thus Frona, the heroine,

---

to the lives of his forbears" (ed. New York, 1912, p. 51). Taken from California into the frozen North — "jerked from the heart of civilization and flung into the heart of things primordial" (p. 43) — he learns fast and is soon clever enough to supplement his meager rations by stealing. London's comment upon this action is illuminating: "This first theft marked Buck as fit to survive in the hostile Northland environment. It marked his adaptability, his capacity to adjust himself to changing conditions, the lack of which would have meant swift and terrible death. It marked, further, the decay or going to pieces of his moral nature, a vain thing and a handicap in the ruthless struggle for existence. It was all well enough in the Southland, under the law of love and fellowship, to respect private property and personal feelings: but in the Northland, under the law of club and fang, whoso took such things into account was a fool, and in so far as he observed them he would fail to prosper" (pp. 59–60). Here the "moral nature" can be thrust aside without the reader's losing respect for Buck. Always it is the life-impulse in him expressing itself. London pauses in a self-conscious digression to explain the nature of this impulse:

"There is an ecstasy that marks the summit of life, and beyond which life cannot rise. And such is the paradox of living, this ecstasy comes when one is most alive, and it comes as a complete forgetfulness [which London himself was obviously never able to achieve] that one is alive. This ecstasy, this forgetfulness of living, comes to the artist, caught up and out of himself in a sheet of flame; it comes to the soldier, war-mad on a stricken field and refusing quarter; and it came to Buck, leading the pack, sounding the old wolf-cry, straining after the food that was alive and that fled swiftly before him through the moonlight" (p. 91).

This is the materialistic philosophy transformed by the celebration of the single vital and inescapable fact which even materialism recognizes as valuable — *life*. Seen from within, the struggle represents the surge of life — and the struggle is dominated by will. It is will in the sense of impulse, life-urge, ecstasy of power — rather than as the ability to exercise a power of ethical choice. It is presented as an animal thing, inherited and consequently not really "free." With a man whom the reader knew as intimately as he knows Buck there would have to be some kind of ethical responsibility. Corliss, as we shall see, is the hero of *A Daughter of the Snows*, regardless of his primordialism, by virtue of his higher moral nature, his honor, loyalty, chastity, and generous patience. But with Buck there need be only this animal expression of the life-instinct that is derived from the "racial memory" of his ancestors within him.

liked the man because he was a man. In her wildest flights she could never imagine linking herself with any man, no matter how exalted spiritually, who was not a man physically. It was a delight to her and a joy to look upon the strong males of her kind, with bodies comely in the sight of God and muscles swelling with the promise of deeds and work. Man, to her, was pre-eminently a fighter. She believed in natural selection and in sexual selection, and was certain that if man had thereby become possessed of faculties and functions, they were for him to use and could but tend to his good. [Observe the ethical and teleological implications that creep in.] And likewise with instincts. If she felt drawn to any person or thing, it was good for her to be so drawn, good for herself. If she felt impelled to joy in a well-built frame and well-shaped muscle, why should she restrain? Why should she not love the body, and without shame? The history of the race, and of all races, sealed her choice with approval. Down all time, the weak and effeminate males had vanished from the world-stage. Only the strong could inherit the earth. She had been born of the strong, and she chose to cast her lot with the strong.[25]

The reader must not think for an instant that this passage authorizes any sort of sexual freedom. The heroine is unwaveringly chaste because, the tone of the book would seem to say, so fine a creature could be nothing else but chaste. A lady of questionable virtue in the story is scarcely allowed to speak to the heroine. In other words, the atavism is safely mixed with the sexual ethics of civilization — a concession partly, perhaps, to be traced to London's understandable concern for the prejudices of his readers. Because of these exigent conventional morals, soul and sensibility are essential to the heroine.

This affection for atavism merges, elsewhere, into a definition of the "will to power" that is startlingly close to the Nietzschean conception. Frona's love of bodily strength — a strength which is accompanied by a higher moral nature that shines through its splendid physical container — is presented as an ethical choice, a choice involving distinction between good and evil, rather than a choice which represents only the force of animal impulse. Her father, mighty trader of the North, expresses an even higher, a Nietzschean concept of will in describing the code of the strong:

Conventions are worthless for such as we. They are for the swine who without them would wallow deeper. The weak must obey or be crushed; not so with the strong. The mass is nothing; the individual everything; and it is the individual, always, that rules the mass and gives the law. A fig for what the world says![26]

These lines almost define the "master morality" of self-assertion that Nietzsche opposed to the miserable "slave morality" by which the

[25] *A Daughter of the Snows*, pp. 86–87. [26] *Ibid.*, p. 184.

weak sought to protect themselves from the strong. Frona, likewise, combines beautiful physique and hardihood with profound intellectual subtlety.   Bred in the North, she has been educated in the United States, and the product is an ideal example, London seems to say, of the higher woman, the superwoman with perfect body and piercing intellect.[27]   In the treatment of the hero the notion of the superman draws markedly away from the Nietzschean concept, the difference being measured by the hero's atavism:

Gambling without stakes is an insipid amusement, and Corliss discovered, likewise, that the warm blood which rises from hygienic gymnasium work is something quite different from that which pounds hotly along when thew matches thew and flesh impacts on flesh and the stake is life and limb. [And in a later conflict,] The din of twenty centuries of battle was roaring in his ear, and the clamor for return to type strong upon him.[28]

It would be difficult to show a rigid logical connection between these ideas which are expressed throughout *A Daughter of the Snows*. A satisfactory classification of them is to consider the determinism to be the conclusion of the calm philosopher who contemplates the flow of life from without; whereas the atavism, the "will-to-power" creed, and the glorying in physical prowess and valiant struggle represent the attitude toward the same set of facts that the intelligent and unscrupulous strong man would take when he found himself embroiled in the conflict. It is the philosophy of a fighter, celebrating will (as vital force, which is thus subjectively identified with ethical rightness), diametrically opposed to the "experimental" calm of a Zola — and yet depending on the same basic assumptions.

Mixed with this wondrous individualism is a good deal of conventional and rather high-flown moral idealism; and this latter element is woven into the structural pattern of the novel even more closely than the idea of ruthless self-assertion. The central complication of the story consists of a triangle: Frona Welse, superwoman, is strongly attracted to Vance Corliss, the full-blooded newcomer to the North who is responding so atavistically to its challenge; but

[27] London does not mention Nietzsche in this novel; nor does he use the word "superman" — what is indicated here is no more than an adumbration of the code of the German philosopher, whose works London appears to have read for the first time about 1905. See p. 104, n. 30.

[28] *A Daughter of the Snows*, pp. 120 and 148. Later Corliss explicitly states the materialistic philosophy of living life for the sake of what can be enjoyed on earth, since nothing afterward is certain (see pp. 220–221).

Frona's heart is ensnared by the guile of one Gregory St. Vincent. Since Corliss is the hero, St. Vincent must be the villain. His villainy consists primarily in the fact that he is a coward and secondarily in the fact that he has become a liar in order to hide his cowardice. The main action of the story is a series of events in which St. Vincent's cowardice is exposed to Frona while Corliss's rugged heroism and loving self-abnegation are given ideal opportunities to display themselves.

The reader will doubtless recognize here the fictional convention which permits the oily-tongued rascal to win his way into the fine woman's heart — while the true hero stands by suffering but inarticulate until the rascal's perfidy catches up with him and exposes (with the aid of the hero) his baseness, leaving the way clear for the good man to claim his reward. In so important a situation, odd though it may seem to the realistic reader, this fictional convention permits the superwoman's judgment to be in error without any shadow being cast upon her shining perfection. This convention, it would appear, rests upon the assumption that wrong will be punished and that a just Providence will always reward patient virtue. It rests upon the assumption, in short, of a moral order, a universe properly controlled in accordance with absolute concepts of justice and right. It is, therefore, diametrically opposed to the materialism which admits no possibility of moral control of the universe. Now although atavism and self-assertion are constantly invoked in *A Daughter of the Snows*, the reader always knows that he is reading steadily toward the final triumph of the moral order through the exposure of St. Vincent and the rich rewarding of Corliss's noble love. The reader knows that the novel will revolve about this vindication of eternal justice, and he is not disappointed. It is for this reason that we say the structural pattern of the novel is woven upon a framework of ethical thought.[29] The Moral Principle

[29] As has been suggested earlier (p. 99, n. 24), *The Call of the Wild* is more successfully naturalistic. It embodies materialism as seen from the point of view of the struggler. Determinism, though latent in materialism, does not emerge as an articulated theory or as a controlling principle of the action, for the emphasis is upon events seen from within the sphere of their influence; but the conflict of animal impulse and ethical nature is successfully evaded because the hero is a dog, of whom ethical action is not expected. Even there, however, the most moving passages are those which deal with Buck's love for his master, Thornton, and which, consequently, appeal strongly to the reader's sense of moral rightness and goodness; and thus, in the last analysis, *The Call of the Wild* is not so essen-

is displayed in operation. Frona's purity is providentially saved
from too intimate contact with the utter baseness of St. Vincent;
and, just as her goodness is manifested in a truly heroic devotion —
in the face of terrific uncertainty — to the man whom she has pledged
her heart, so Providence rises to the occasion with a magnificent
exposure that resolves all her doubts. Even though the belief in this
moral order may have come to London as a bit of story-writing
technique, as a pattern, that is, which had been employed in countless
earlier novels, it is used in a way that makes the writer's acceptance
of it unquestionable. It is the mainspring of the action; and its
presence indicates how very slightly London was able to make his
determinism carry the burden of his plot.[30]

---

tially different from *A Daughter of the Snows*. In its action, moreover, it evades
ethical motivation not by using deterministic motivation but because it is *episodic*,
having no carefully articulated plot conflict.

[30] *The Sea-Wolf* (1904) contains a sharper divergence of these tendencies
toward moral idealism and egotistical self-assertion. In *A Daughter of the Snows*
these contradictory impulses are drawing gently apart; in *The Sea-Wolf* they
have rushed to opposite poles, and it is matter for wonder that they have remained within the bounds of a single novel.

The ostensible hero is Humphrey Van Weyden, a gentlemanly dilettante
who has been rescued from a wreck and carried off on a sealing vessel. But the
unquestionable center of interest in the first third of the book is Wolf Larsen,
captain of the sealer, strong, brutal, brilliant. The plot complication begins
with the addition (from another wreck) of a fragile poetess to the ship's company.
Humphrey loves Maud, the poetess. Wolf too is attracted by her, and her
danger resolves the story into a clash between heartless egotism and ethical
idealism. The first half of the novel sets the stage for a conflict which is suddenly
avoided by the escape of the lovers, over a stormy sea, to an undiscovered seal
island in northern waters. The story of Wolf Larsen might, if carried to a natural
and consistent end, take him through a number of fierce encounters into a climax
in which he could be killed, or could triumph over, say, the rival sealers and
become a Titan of the seas. Certainly the story of the hardfisted superman
should be told from a consistent point of view. This is especially true since
Wolf is the unquestionable hero of the first third of the book. It is worse than
inept to direct the reader's sympathies toward a particular character and then
abandon him in favor of another character, with another story, seen from another
point of view. The second part of the story — or rather the second story —
takes place upon the seal island. Again there is no conflict between the representatives of ethical control and of "primitive" ruthlessness. Humphrey does
not meet and destroy Larsen; he barely evades him until Larsen is stricken by
a mysterious paralysis. Wolf Larsen is an ominous shadow that hangs over the
lovers; his personality still carries great weight, but his function is spectacular
rather than structural. His being destroyed by some secret malady necessarily
prevents his destruction by the working out of a plot complication. Seen in this
light *The Sea-Wolf* tells the love story of Humphrey and Maud; and in that
story Wolf is an elaborate *decoration*. He is the volcano in the shadow of which

Further evidence of the idealism which is mixed with London's materialism is the fact that Frona and Corliss are sexually chaste,

the lovers meet, struggle, and finally achieve happiness as the volcano gradually becomes extinct. Like a volcano's, Wolf's failure is inward and — to outward seeming — uncaused.

In the face of this evidence we come upon the statement, made later by London, of the meaning of *The Sea-Wolf:* "I want to make a tale so plain that he who runs may read, and then there is the underlying psychological motif. In 'The Sea Wolf' there was, of course, the superficial descriptive story, while the underlying tendency was to prove that the superman cannot be successful in modern life. The superman is anti-social in his tendencies, and in these days of our complex society and sociology he cannot be successful in his hostile aloofness. Hence the unpopularity of the financial superman like Rockefeller; he acts like an irritant in the social body." *The Book of Jack London,* II : 57. The passage dates from after the composition of the novel, probably from the summer of 1905. Now in the novel itself there is no use of the word "superman" and, although there is reference to Darwin, Huxley, Tyndall, and others, there is no mention of Nietzsche. It would appear that London was expatiating *ex post facto* in the statement of intention quoted above. Charmian London (*op. cit.,* II : 31–33) tells of Jack's bringing her volumes of Nietzsche in the summer of 1905. He speaks of himself at that time as "getting hold of some of Nietzsche" — and the probable conclusion to be drawn from these statements is that 1905 marks London's *first* acquaintance with Nietzsche's works. Thereafter he mentions him at every opportunity, and it is hard to imagine that anything besides ignorance could have kept him from using the magic name in *The Sea-Wolf.*

Our preliminary discussion of the superman, real or fancied, shows that London's Wolf Larsen, a mixture of egotism, cruelty, "atavism," and disillusionment, is not a genuine Nietzschean superman. Furthermore, the contention that "the superman cannot be successful in modern life" — assuming for the moment that Wolf is a true superman — cannot be said to have been demonstrated through the movement of the novel, for instead of being destroyed by social forces shown at work in the plot, he is destroyed by an unknown and adventitious something within him that could hardly be shown to represent society's hostility to his kind. It was equally inept to imply that Rockefeller could not be successful in modern life, and a novel in which Rockefeller died of brain tumor after accumulating his billions would hardly demonstrate how he was unfitted to survive in society.

The structural form of *The Sea-Wolf* is conventional, though its content and setting are unusual. The movement of its plot depends upon acts of will and in no sense embodies the operation of external determining forces. Wolf Larsen is the person who sees nature's determinism as acting upon himself and hence, recognizing no values or laws but those of his own life-impulse or "will," acts upon a program of complete selfishness. This can be called naturalism only if the word is used in a special sense. It is materialism transformed by the American frontier. It is a kind of naturalism that celebrates rather than denies the will; it has no particular effect upon the structural pattern of the novel; it does not bring the operation of determinism into the novel's movement; in short, it brings decoration in the shape of a curious philosophy and a striking character in the person of Wolf, into a novel whose spokesman and hero stands for the ethical point of view.

whereas St. Vincent is known to be otherwise. The thoroughgoing materialist would not blame a man for acting upon his natural impulses; rather he would encourage such activity. London, of course, was writing books to sell, and he always worked to please his reader; but it is nevertheless significant that he should slide so easily into the grooves of conventional thinking. And the story makes the most of the moral ardor which is kindled by its situations; the final scene is devoted to the heroine's icy denunciation of the miserable lying coward:

> "Shall I tell you why, Gregory St. Vincent?" she said again. "Tell you why your kisses have cheapened me? Because you broke the faith of food and blanket. Because you broke salt with a man, and then watched that man fight unequally for life without lifting your hand. Why, I had rather you had died in defending him; the memory of you would have been good. Yes, I had rather you had killed him yourself. At least, it would have shown there was blood in your body." [31]

The novel, to conclude, is built around acts of free will and based upon an implicit faith in a moral order. In these respects London's determinism has not penetrated to its structure. In two other respects, however, it has done so. In the first place, the action as described above takes up only a small part of the novel. In the rest of it, accompanying the digressive exposition of philosophical materialism, are scene after scene in which the conditions of Alaskan life are depicted. Gold-hunting, starvation, the rigors of the trail, the awesome spectacle of an ice pack breaking up, are some of the many sequences which fill its pages. In this picturesque presentation of the frozen North one sees the *conditions* under which the struggle for existence, as naïvely conceived by London, is carried on. They are conditions which challenge man's strength and courage. They are not part of the plot proper of *A Daughter of the Snows*, but they do account for a large part of its content.

The other point at which London's naturalism enters is in his choice of cowardice as the hallmark of villainy. Cowardice argues unfitness in the struggle for existence more directly than dishonesty, deceit, or any of the "moral" failings which would impair a man's status in a more civilized community. But London brings what can only be called moral ardor to his championship of the clean, rugged, he-man virtues he values so highly. Cowardice in this

---

[31] *A Daughter of the Snows*, p. 333.

story is regarded as the most loathsome of sins — so loathsome that one is led to experience powerful moral indignation at the thought of its embodiment being married to Frona Welse. In this way the moral and the amoral are intertwined.

This analysis should demonstrate the inadequacy of Mr. Hartwick's definition of naturalism.[32] A writer like London does not invent supermen whom he allows to express themselves amorally through a code of complete *laissez faire*. His characters are praised or condemned for their adherence to a code of ethics as rigid as that of bourgeois society. This code of ethics continually interfered with his avowed materialism so that not only was he unable to write novels which pretended, like Zola's, to display in their structure and movement the deterministic operation of natural or social law; he was also unable, when he viewed his materialism through the eyes of the struggler for existence, to free himself from ethical presuppositions which entered and controlled his plots at every turn. The resulting combination of survival materialism with the high-flown moral propriety of the genteel 1900's wrenches nearly all of London's novels into strange and illogical patterns.

UNIVERSITY OF OKLAHOMA
NORMAN, OKLAHOMA

[32] See p. 94.

Printed in the United States
134296LV00003B/75/A

9 781432 626969